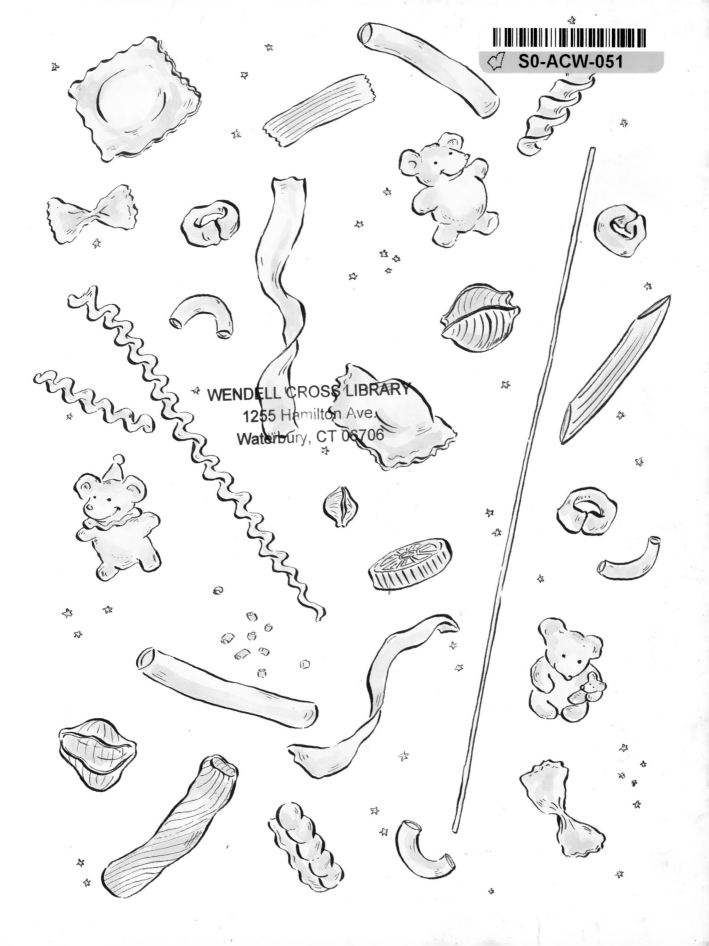

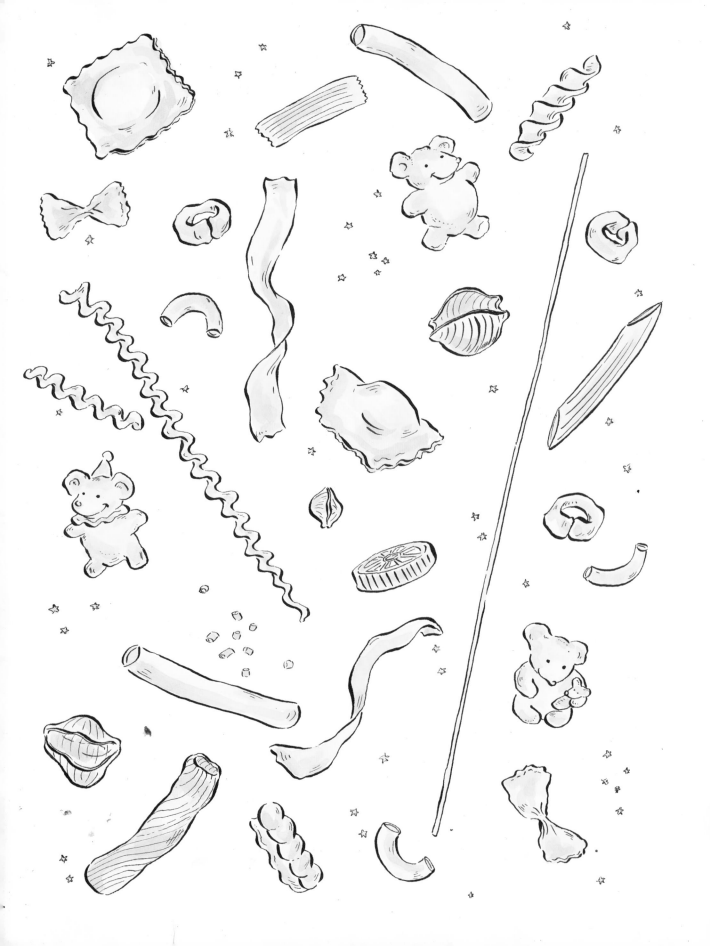

GINO BADINO

For the Wendell L. Cross School —

DIANA ENGEL

Happy Reading!

Morrow Junior Books / New York

Diana Engel

For my daughters, Maria and Luisa

Watercolors and black ink were used for the full-color art.
The text type is 14 point Caxton Light.

Copyright © 1991 by Diana Engel

Printed in Singapore at Tien Wah Press.

1 2 3 4 5 6 7 8 9 10

Library of Congress Cataloging-in-Publication Data
Engel, Diana.
Gino Badino / Diana Engel.
p.   cm.
Summary: Gino would rather sculpt mice out of dough than sweep the
floor in his family's pasta factory, but when the factory falls on
hard times, Gino's mice save the day.
ISBN 0-688-09502-X. —ISBN 0-688-09503-8 (lib. bdg.)
[1. Pasta products—Fiction.   2. Factories—Fiction.
3. Sculptors—Fiction.   4. Family life—Fiction.]   I. Title.
PZ7.E69874Gi   1991
[E]—dc20   90-36456   CIP   AC

For as long as anyone could remember, the Badino family had been making pasta—spinach pasta, egg pasta, carrot, and tomato.

The family factory was a bustling, busy place where
everyone had a special job...even Gino, the youngest Badino.
His job was to sweep the factory floor each day after school.

Gino hated his job and looked for any excuse not to do it.

One day, he picked up a nice-looking piece of dough and squeezed it through his fingers. "This stuff is great!" he said. "It feels like clay!"

"Don't forget your sweeping," said Mama as she mixed just the right amount of flour and water and eggs.

"And when you're finished," said Grandma, testing a new recipe, "come taste this...broccoli pasta!"

But Gino had other things in mind. He twisted and molded the piece of dough until he found the right shape.

In the morning, his little mouse was hard and dry. Now I'll try something a little bigger, he thought.

Each day, Gino picked up bits and pieces of discarded
dough. He loved feeling the softness take shape in his hands.
He made all sorts of creatures, but his favorites were the mice.

His fingers always busy, Gino watched his family work.

"I wish you'd remember to collect your little friends," said his sister, Leonora.

"Me, too!" said Uncle Dom, poring over the list of stores that sold Badino pasta.

Gino had trouble remembering..

But while he played, his fingers grew more sure, his ideas more wonderful.

"What's this?" cried Mama at bath time. "More dough?"

Gino was so busy, he didn't even hear.

Soon Gino's friends were treated to special birthday gifts...

and Gino's creations were the hit of Show and Tell.

In fact, the art teacher thought Gino's work deserved a
special display of its own.

But at home, the thing that Gino liked to do best only got him into trouble.

"Every day you sit there playing with dough!" his father would shout. "Where's the broom? Where's the dustpan? You've got work to do!"

Now, the Badinos were a kind family and they loved their
little Gino very much. But they had to work hard to keep
their business going. They had no time for Gino's macaroni
animals and fancy shapes.

Late one night, Gino heard voices outside his bedroom door.

"Our little business is not doing well," said Uncle Dom. "The big companies can make more pasta in one hour than we can make in one day!"

"Aagh!" said Grandma. "That stuff tastes like cardboard!"

"I know," said Mama, "but if they make more pasta, they can sell it for less."

"Then," said Papa, "we'll make more pasta and sell ours for less, too!"

"But how can we work harder than we do now?" asked Uncle Dom. They all sat at the table in gloomy silence.

Gino called out to his father. "I can help," he said. "Give me
a real job, and I know I can help."

"When you are bigger, my little linguine," said Papa.
"When you are bigger."

In the morning, Gino was up early. He ran downstairs to the factory.

"I'll show them I can do a real job," he muttered. "We need more pasta? I'll make more pasta!"

Grabbing bags of flour and cartons of eggs, Gino began to fill the great pasta machine.

He pushed the button and waited for the smooth, flat sheets of dough to roll out.

At first, nothing happened. Then there was a loud belching noise. There was another belch, a squeak, a huge grunt...

...and an enormous explosion!

Like a volcano, the machine spit out a great gush of dough,
sending it so high that golden pasta rained all over the
factory floor.

To Gino, it was all quite beautiful.

The machine was quiet. He could hear his family stomping down the stairs.

Gino knew he was in big trouble.

"Gino!" shouted Papa. "What have you done?"
"What a mess!" cried Mama. "What a mess!"
"That boy had better grow up fast," said Grandma.
Uncle Dom picked up a mop. "Let's get to work," he said.
"We've got to get another shipment out or we're really sunk."

The Badinos worked frantically, all day and all night.

In the confusion, a few mistakes were made.

Finally, a new shipment of pasta was ready for Uncle
Dom's truck.

Gino, who hadn't touched a piece of dough since the
explosion, swept quietly. Something odd in one of the boxes
caught his eye.

"Oh no!" he groaned. A Gino Badino macaroni mouse stared happily from the window of the box.

Gino didn't dare say a word.

A week later, at the end of a busy day, there was a knock at the door. It was the owner of a store that sold Badino pasta.

"Is there something wrong?" asked Mama.

"I've come about those macaroni mice," he said.

Mama stared at him, bewildered.

The store owner smiled. "You know, the ones that were packed in that last shipment. There was a clown mouse and a cowboy mouse—"

"Gino!" Papa shouted. He looked like the pasta machine about to explode.

"Oh, so this is the artist," said the man. "Great idea! Very creative! Every box is sold. Now everyone wants to collect those little creatures. I can sell as many as you've got! When's the next shipment?"

Papa opened his mouth, but nothing came out.

"Right away," said Grandma quickly, "right away!"

After the man left, Gino looked at his father. At first, nothing happened. Then Papa laughed so loud, the windows shook. Soon all the Badinos were laughing. Gino laughed longer than anyone.

"Well, son," said Papa, "you've got a big job tomorrow."

The next afternoon, Papa picked up the broom.
"You've got more important things to do than sweeping,"
he said. "I want to see some more of those famous macaroni
mice!"

Gino was truly happy. His afternoons were full of real
work.
And his nights were full of pasta.